WILD RESCUE

POLAR MELTDOWN

FOR POLAR BEARS INTERNATIONAL
FOR ALL THEIR IMPORTANT
WORK ON BEHALF OF THESE
MAGNIFICENT ANIMALS – JB & SV

STRIPES PUBLISHING
An imprint of Magi Publications
1 The Coda Centre, 189 Munster Road,
London SW6 6AW

A paperback original
First published in Great Britain in 2009

ISBN: 978-1-84715-067-7

WILD
RESCUE
POLAR MELTDOWN

J. Burchett and S. Vogler

Stripes

STATUS: LIVE
LOCATION:
ALASKA, USA
CODENAME: SNOW WHITE

WILD

STATUS: FILE CLOSED
LOCATION:
SICHUAN, CHINA
CODE NAME: JING JING

STATUS: FILE CLOSED
LOCATION:
SOUTH BORNEO
CODE NAME: KAWAN

STATUS: FILE CLOSED
LOCATION:
SUMATRA, INDONESIA
CODE NAME: TORA

RESCUE

MISSION DATABASE

CHAPTER ONE

"Finished before you!" declared Zoe, hitting enter on the keyboard in front of her. Her result flashed up on the screen: "Animal print identification quiz – 49 out of 50. Congratulations, Wild Operative Zoe Woodward!"

"I've got them *all* right," boasted Ben, her twin brother, as he finished seconds after her. He looked at Zoe's results. "Fancy not knowing the shape of the moose hoof!"

"Well, it's hard," protested Zoe. "All the deer prints are so alike. I had to guess."

Ben grinned. "So did I," he admitted.
He pushed his chair back and looked round
at the state-of-the-art education centre,
with its row of computer terminals and
huge resource area full of books and
manuals, maps and charts. "This place is so
cool," he said. "In fact, everything we've
done here at Wild HQ has been awesome.
The climbing wall was the best."

"The water sports were my favourite," said
Zoe. "Especially the canoeing."

Ben and Zoe were very unusual eleven-
year-olds. They were the youngest operatives
in Wild, a top-secret organization dedicated
to saving endangered animals. The head of
the organization, their godfather Dr Stephen
Fisher, had invited them to spend the Easter
holidays at his headquarters hidden deep
underground on a remote island. They'd
been undertaking a series of exercises to
sharpen up their physical and mental skills

for future Wild missions – endurance challenges, advanced satellite tracking and finally a series of brain boggling tests.

"I'll be sorry to go back home," said Zoe.

"We've had a great time," agreed Ben. "I wish we could stay longer."

The door slid open and the lanky figure of Uncle Stephen appeared. He was wearing a white lab coat, a straw hat and bright stripy shorts. Zoe tried not to giggle.

"Well done, Ben and Zoe," he said. "You've passed all your challenges with flying colours. Just one last little identification test."

He tossed them a glass eye. Ben snatched it out of the air before Zoe could get her hands on it. They looked at each other in excitement. They knew what the eye meant. They weren't going home after all. Uncle Stephen must have a new rescue mission for them!

They peered at the eyeball. This was their uncle's little clue to get them to guess the animal in danger.

"It's dark," said Ben, "and the pupil's huge."

"Looks like my old teddy bear's eye," joked Zoe.

"You're getting close," said Dr Fisher.

"The most endangered bear I can think of is the polar bear," said Ben.

"Quite right!" Their godfather beamed. "And I've got a bear or two in the Arctic that need your help. Come with me to the Control Room."

Ben and Zoe followed him eagerly along the corridor to the Control Room and placed their fingertips on the ID pad.

"Print identification complete," came the electronic voice.

The door swung open to reveal the centre of Wild's Headquarters – a brightly-lit room full of operatives at flashing control panels and busy computer screens.

Uncle Stephen went over to a touch screen and brought up an Internet blog. "This was posted today," he told them. "It's from a vet in an Inupiat community in Fairwood, Alaska. I often read Theo Airut's entries because he sounds a decent bloke who cares for the animals in the area. And it keeps me up to date with events out there. Erika has set the computer to flag up any problems and this certainly got the alarm bells ringing – well, we don't have actual alarm bells of course, far too noisy."

Zoe read the blog aloud. "'A local man brought the body of a polar bear into the village today.'" She sighed. "How sad!"

Ben scrolled down the entry. "'He'd gone out on a fishing expedition and the bear attacked him. He had to shoot it to save his own life. Then he brought the body back for its fur.'"

"Theo asked to see the body," Uncle Stephen told them. "He's posted several recent entries about the bears not getting enough to eat and he wanted to check this one out. It's very unusual for a polar bear to attack a human, but this one appears to have been starving." He looked grave. "I'm afraid global warming is taking its toll on their numbers. I'm sure you've heard all about the polar ice cap getting thinner."

Ben and Zoe nodded.

"Seals normally build their birth lairs in the thick ice shelves, but because the ice has been thinner these last few years the seals can't breed as well."

"And seals are the main source of food for polar bears," said Zoe.

"Indeed." Uncle Stephen nodded. "The seals are full of fat, which in turn gives the polar bear a thick fat layer. This keeps them warm and enables them to go without food for long periods."

"Wait a minute," said Ben, puzzled. "If this bear's already dead, what's our mission?"

"The vet's examination showed something particularly worrying," Uncle Stephen continued. "The dead bear was a lactating female."

"That's awful!" gasped Zoe. "It means there could be motherless cubs out there in the wild."

"The Arctic can be a very hostile terrain," said Dr Fisher. "This mission will be your most difficult yet. You need to find those cubs before it's too late."

CHAPTER TWO

Ben and Zoe gazed at each other in excitement. This was like nothing they'd ever done before.

"Any clues to where we should look?" asked Zoe.

"The blogger didn't say where the bear attacked," said Uncle Stephen. "That's something you'll have to find out when you get there."

"I don't suppose she would have strayed far from her cubs," said Ben thoughtfully. "Polar bears build birthing dens, don't they?

They make them in the snow on the land and stay in them for months."

"They do," said Uncle Stephen.

"So we find out where the attack took place and start our search there," said Zoe.

"Exactly," said Uncle Stephen. "Most bears give birth in December and January – usually to twins – and when the cubs are about two or three months old they start bringing them out. So our little orphans could have started exploring, but they'll still be dependent on their mum for milk."

The door opened and a smiling young woman with a ponytail came in. It was Erika Bohn, Dr Fisher's second in command.

"I've just got the latest weather reports for Fairwood," she told them. "Minus twenty degrees centigrade with snow showers."

"Minus twenty!" gasped Zoe. "That's incredibly cold. And won't it be dark most of the time?"

"It would be in the depths of winter," Erika explained. "But as it's March there'll be about twelve hours of daylight, like here."

She tapped a screen and brought up a map of the Arctic Circle.

"Here's Fairwood," she said, zooming in on the northern coast of Alaska. "That's the village where the fisherman lives. I'll take you there so you can find out more from him. Eager questions from a couple of kids won't look suspicious. I'm going to pretend to be your mother and we'll be tourists."

"Then you two will head off to search for the bear cubs while Erika goes further along the coast," put in Uncle Stephen.

"There's a new oil drilling project being proposed in the Arctic near to Fairwood," Erika told them. "We're fearful that pollution from the drilling will add to the problems that global warming is already causing for the animals there. I'm going to investigate."

"You'll be needing my latest invention, of course," said Uncle Stephen, proudly pulling out a small crate from under a workstation and rummaging around inside. "I'm very excited about my RAT."

With a flourish, their godfather pulled out two streamlined snowboards with micro-sized engines at the back. They were about half the size of a normal skateboard and folded in half for packing. The children had never seen anything like them.

"The RAT," he explained. "The Rapid Arctic Traveller. I've made them from a special ultra-bonded polyurethane I've developed. They're so strong an elephant could use them – if it could get its feet in the footholds. And the beauty is they're made entirely from recycled materials."

He placed one on the ground and stood on it, kicking the engine into life with his heel.

"Dr Fisher!" warned Erika. "Remember what happened last time you tried it out."

"I thought I'd be safe in the corridor," protested Uncle Stephen, as the RAT wobbled dangerously. "I didn't know that James was about to come out of the staff restaurant with a tray of yoghurts."

"I wish I'd seen that!" said Ben.

"I rather resembled a milkshake afterwards," admitted their godfather, reluctantly stepping off the RAT.

"It's just like skateboarding," said Erika. "And I know you two are experts at that. The RAT power-glides across the snow. It's very flexible and copes with bumpy terrain. The engine runs on batteries, solar powered of course, and it will keep going for forty-eight hours without a boost."

"Awesome!" gasped Ben.

"I can't wait to try it out," exclaimed Zoe, taking one in her hands. "It's so light."

"And now for the rest of your equipment," said Erika. "You'll be needing your BUGs and suitable clothing." She opened a drawer and handed them two small devices. The BUGs, short for Brilliant Undercover Gizmos, looked like handheld games consoles to anyone who didn't know. They were, in fact,

sophisticated machines that did a whole
range of things from satellite mapping to
animal tracking.

"I wouldn't want to go without this," said
Ben, scrolling through the menu.

Uncle Stephen chuckled. "Don't forget
to pack your long johns – they'll be just as
vital as your BUGs on this chilly mission."

Erika led Ben and Zoe over to the
stockroom.

The Wild stockroom was an Aladdin's
cave of marvellous technological devices,
clothes for every possible climate, and
various half-finished inventions of Uncle
Stephen's full of wires and springs.

Erika pulled two backpacks off a shelf.
"I've already put a tent in one of these,"
she told them. "And your ultra-light
thermal sleeping bags." She then took two
baby bottles and some powdered milk from
a wall cupboard.

"This is specially formulated to match the rich milk of a polar bear mother," she said. "Now pass those white bundles, please, Zoe."

"What are they?" asked Zoe, pulling two furry fleeces out of a box.

"Slings," said Uncle Stephen, appearing in the doorway. "When you find the cubs you'll need something to carry them in. They'll be about the size of large cats by now. The fur will make them think you're their mother. We don't want them to get used to humans."

The children stashed the slings in their backpacks, and Dr Fisher showed them the special side pockets that kept the folded RATs hidden from view. Erika made two piles of clothes for them to take.

"Looks as if Erika's getting you to pack everything but the kitchen sink!" laughed Uncle Stephen. "She's right though.

You must be prepared for the worst the weather can throw at you out there."

Erika grinned at him as she picked up two pairs of goggles.

"These are specially designed for the Arctic," she said. "They act as snow goggles, which you will find essential, but when you press the logo here…" she touched the small symbol on one side and immediately the lower half of the glass darkened, "…that part becomes thermogoggles."

Erika handed the goggles to Ben and Zoe.

"Awesome!" said Ben.

Ben and Zoe hoisted their backpacks on to their shoulders and slung their Arctic clothing over their arms.

"We're ready!" declared Zoe.

"Good luck," said Uncle Stephen. "I'll start looking for somewhere that takes polar bear orphans."

Ben turned to face Zoe. "Come on, what are we waiting for? We've got bear cubs to save!"

CHAPTER THREE

Erika brought the aeroplane down on the landing strip of the little airport at Fairwood, Alaska. It was a bright morning and the sun glinted on the snow that lay all around.

"It's eleven o'clock here," said Ben. "So the flight was only seven hours! This is a fantastic plane."

"Your uncle's very pleased with his new design." Erika smiled as she took off the pilot's headset. "It's all made from recycled products, but it still looks like an ordinary private jet. You're the first passengers."

"I see he's still using chicken poo in his special fuel," said Zoe, wrinkling her nose.

Everything at Wild was run on eco-friendly – but rather pongy – fuels.

"But there's something else," added Ben. "It doesn't quite smell the same."

"Well spotted," said Erika. "He put egg yolks in the mixture. That makes for a much more efficient fuel."

"Certainly makes it faster!" said Zoe.

They picked up their bulging backpacks.

"Hats, gloves, everything on before I open the door," instructed Erika. "And don't take anything off while you're outside. Frostbite can hit in minutes."

The children were wearing fleecy tracksuits and long underwear. Now they zipped themselves into white padded waterproof trousers and jackets, and pulled on their balaclavas and gloves.

"Warm as toast!" Ben grinned.

They stepped down on to the tarmac. Their breath made clouds in the freezing air.

"It's so cold!" gasped Zoe, looking round the desolate airstrip with its single building that rose from the flat snow all around. "The air's even freezing the inside of my nose!" She tried not to think about the poor cubs huddled in their den, waiting in vain for their mother to return.

"Follow me," said Erika briskly, heading off towards the airport offices. "Once we're through passport control our taxi will be arriving to take us to the Inupiat Heritage Center. It's a good starting place to find out the information we need."

They were soon waiting outside the airport. In the distance across the white landscape they could just make out a cluster of houses.

Ben was peering down the snow-covered road, marked out by its row of telegraph poles. "I think I've just spotted our taxi," he said, "and it's awesome!"

Zoe gasped as she followed his gaze.
A large sledge was gliding towards them,
pulled by a team of eager huskies. The
sledge drew alongside and the huskies stood
panting as a short, stocky man dressed in
fur-trimmed animal skin jumped down.

"Miss Bohn?" he enquired with a broad smile.

Erika smiled back and nodded. "And these are my children, Ben and Zoe."

"Welcome to Alaska," said the man. He spoke with an American accent. "My name's Charlie."

Ben and Zoe went over and admired the sledge.

"This is going to be great!" exclaimed Zoe. "Shall we get in, Mum?"

The children gave each other a secret grin. They were used to Erika taking on different roles for their missions, but it was funny to pretend she was their mother.

"Oh course, dear," Erika replied. "But no pushing and shoving."

The children scrambled aboard, settled themselves on the long bench and covered their legs with a blanket.

Zoe kept her eye on the dogs. One of them looked younger and fluffier than the others and it was rolling in the snow, getting tangled in its chain.

"How sweet!" She sighed. "I just want to hug it."

"Zoe's having an attack of gooeyness," groaned Ben.

"Leave your sister alone," said Erika, rolling her eyes at Charlie.

They watched him say a few sharp words to the dog.

"That one's just finished her training," he told them, as he climbed into the sledge. "She'll be really good when she settles down."

One or two of the huskies were already howling in their impatience to get going, and he urged them forwards with some words the children didn't understand. The sledge glided over the snow in a wide arc and then set off in its previous tracks.

The landscape was very flat and the snow lay deep and undisturbed. One solitary bare tree was growing on a small mound.

In spite of his warm clothes, Ben gave a shiver. This was like nothing he'd experienced before. The coldest place he and Zoe had ever been was Austria on a family skiing holiday. And then they'd been able to

go back to a cosy hotel when they got cold.
Who knew what lay ahead of them on this
mission? No roaring fires for certain once
they'd embarked on their search.

"Do you go everywhere on dog sledges?"
Zoe asked the driver.

Charlie grinned at her. "Only when I'm
transporting tourists," he said. "We know
you like to see the old way of life of the
Inupiat people – which is why I dress in
the traditional way. We have motorized
sledges for everyday."

"Cool!" exclaimed Ben. "But what
do the dogs do then?"

"There are enough tourists to keep
them busy," chuckled Charlie. As the
sledge took a bend, a vast sparkling
expanse of ice came into view, broken
by small channels of dark water. "The
Arctic Ocean," their driver announced.

The sledge joined a wider road and
eventually they came to a short main street
of shops and a couple of restaurants. Other
roads branched away, lined with single
storey houses painted in bright colours.

At the far end of the street the driver urged the dogs through a gateway. They stopped outside a large, grey brick building with a gently sloping snow-covered roof. It stood right on the shore of the ocean. A row of flags flapped in the freezing wind. Among them Ben recognized the deep blue of the Alaskan flag with its rich yellow stars.

"That's the North Star," he said, pointing at the largest star, "and the Plough constellation – also known as the Great Bear."

"OK, show off!" Zoe laughed. "But the Great Bear's just right for our mission," she added in a whisper.

They jumped out of the sledge and Erika paid Charlie. The children gazed in awe at a huge skull displayed on a plinth outside.

"Look at that!" gasped Ben. "It's as big as a car!"

"That's from a bowhead whale," explained

Charlie. "You'll find out all about the history of whaling inside."

Although she tried to hide it, Ben caught a glimpse of Zoe's disapproving expression.

"I bet that was hunted," she said under her breath.

"We have to accept it's a different way of life," he muttered to her. "The Inupiat rely on whale hunting for food and income."

"I know," Zoe replied, "but it just seems so cruel."

Ben turned back to Charlie. "We were hoping to talk to the fisherman who got attacked by a polar bear," he said. "Do you know where we can find him?"

"Lukie's getting famous!" said the driver. "You might find him inside. He works here when he's not out fishing. He looks after our whaling display."

They thanked him and pushed open the swing doors to the centre. The welcome warm air hit them straight away. They left coats, balaclavas and backpacks in the cloakroom and took in their surroundings.

The centre was a huge, open-plan building

with cabinets full of Inupiat traditional dress and cooking utensils. Beautifully crafted harpoons and kayaks were suspended on wires from the ceiling, and photographs of whaling expeditions past and present stretched along one wall.

Ben made straight for the café in the corner and began to eye up the menu.

"You can't be hungry," said his sister. "You finished off all the sandwiches *and* had a whole pizza on the plane.

"That was ages ago!" protested Ben. "I'm starving."

"We have to find the fisherman first," insisted Zoe.

A woman was stacking postcards into slots on a stand. Zoe went up to her.

"Excuse me," she said. "We heard about a man who got attacked by a bear. We'd like to hear his story. Is he in today?"

The woman put down the postcards.

"You mean Lukie," she said. "That young man's always taking risks. Now everyone's talking about his narrow escape. I haven't seen him this morning."

"What about Theo Airut?" asked Zoe. "It was his blog that told us all about the attack. Perhaps we could speak to him instead."

The woman looked surprised at Zoe's persistence.

"We're doing a school project on polar bears," Ben explained quickly.

"That's why you're so keen," said the woman. "There are plenty of people here who've seen polar bears, but most of us keep our distance!" She nodded to Erika. "It's nice to see kids so keen on schoolwork. You must be proud of them."

"I am," said Erika. "They never let me down."

"Aw, Mum," protested Ben. "You're so embarrassing."

"Do you know where Lukie was when the attack happened?" Zoe asked the woman.

"We want to draw a map for our project and mark the exact spot," added Ben. "It'll make it more exciting to read."

"I wish I could help," said the woman, "but I don't think he said."

"Would Mr Airut know?" asked Zoe.

"He's not here," said the saleswoman.

"He's gone to Anchorage for a few days for a conference." She smiled. "We're a small community – we all know each other's business." She saw the children's disappointed faces. "Are you sticking around?" They nodded. "Lukie should be in later."

"What do we do now?" asked Ben when they'd thanked her and walked out of earshot.

"Time to eat," said Erika.

Ben rubbed his hands together eagerly at the thought of dinner.

"I'm going to find somewhere quiet to contact Dr Fisher for an update on the oil drilling project," Erika added in a low voice. "Will you be all right on your own, children?" she said out loud, as the saleswoman walked by.

"Of course we will, Mum!" declared Ben, pretending to be offended at the question.

"Try and behave yourselves," said Erika, as

she headed off for the cloakroom.

After a plate of fried herring and a giant chocolate chip muffin, the children walked round the displays of whaling memorabilia. They pretended to be deeply engrossed in the exhibits, but glanced around eagerly every time someone came into the centre. Not one of them looked like a local young man.

"Time's running out," said Zoe anxiously. "Those babies are not going to survive long without their mother."

CHAPTER FOUR

"We're not giving up," said Ben. "See that sign by the door. There's traditional igloo and boat building going on outside. Someone else might know Lukie's story and have the information we want."

They pulled on their coats, gloves and balaclavas, then pushed open the swing door and stepped into the bitter air. A freezing wind blew round them making the flags flap violently. They could hear the ice cracking against the shore as the grey waves washed it in.

"Look at this," gasped Zoe, staring at a display board that showed maps of the Arctic and the changes that had occurred over the years. "Thirty years ago there was about three times as much old ice as there is now."

"What's old ice?" asked Ben.

"Old ice is the permanent Arctic ice cap," said Zoe. "And according to this it's getting smaller very quickly." She read aloud: "'Each year it's replaced with newer, thinner ice that melts more easily in the summer.'"

"That's not good news for the polar bears," said Ben. "There'll be even fewer seals to eat."

They walked on through an arch made of whale rib bones. Ben strode ahead along a cleared path to a circle of snow bricks. An old man in traditional dress was squatting by it, cutting more bricks with a long knife. His thick black hair, threaded with white,

stuck out from under his hood. He looked
up and nodded as the children approached.

"Cool!" exclaimed Ben. "I didn't realize
people made igloos any more."

The old man shook his head. "Not many
of us learn how to do it these days," he said.

The children could hear the American in his voice, but they could tell from his accent that English was not his first language. "Eskimos like me used to build igloos when they travelled many miles over the ice to hunt."

"Eskimos?" exclaimed Zoe. "But I thought we weren't supposed to call you that."

The old man's lined face broke into a grin. "You've heard it's an insult to our people. It is not used in Canada, but here in Alaska we are proud to call ourselves Inupiat Eskimos. Though of course you can call me by my name, Amaguq."

"How long does it take to build an igloo?" asked Ben eagerly. "I've always wanted to have a go."

"We haven't got time to chat," Zoe muttered to Ben. But Amaguq was obviously pleased to talk to visitors about his craft.

"For a skilled worker like me, a few

hours," said the man. While he talked he cut a new block and trimmed it with an expert hand so that it fitted neatly on the igloo wall. It was just like watching a bricklayer at home, thought Ben.

"An igloo made a perfect shelter for hunters who were away for weeks on the ice," said the man. He put his knife down. "Of course, if they needed shelter in a hurry they'd dig a snow hole in a bank. Much quicker."

"Are they easier to build?" asked Ben.

Amaguq grinned. "Much easier. You just dig. With the entrance away from the wind if possible – and you mustn't forget to make an air hole."

This was all very interesting, thought Zoe, but it wasn't getting them any closer to finding out where the bear had been killed. The whole purpose of coming out here was to find someone who knew Lukie's story.

"That's fantastic," she said, as the old man finished speaking. "Maybe we can put it in our project. We're studying this area," she explained. "And you might be able to help us with something. We'd like to write about Lukie, the fisherman who works here – the one who was attacked by the polar bear."

"Do you know where it happened, Amaguq?" Ben joined in.

"You'd have to ask Lukie that," said the old Eskimo.

"We'd love to talk to him," said Zoe. "But he's not around at the moment."

"He's sure to be in soon," the man replied. "He promised to repair one of the old canoes in the whaling display."

"So he's not out fishing?" asked Ben.

"Not today, there's a snowstorm forecast for later." Amaguq picked up his knife and began to cut another snow brick.

The children thanked him and retraced

their steps towards the Heritage Centre.

"Glad the weather's stopped Lukie going fishing," said Ben. "Otherwise we might have had to wait ages to speak to him."

"True," said Zoe, frowning. "But there's one thing you've forgotten. *We're* the ones who might be out when the snowstorm hits."

"We'll be all right," Ben said cheerfully. "We've got our tent."

They got to the door of the centre.

"Fingers crossed Lukie's arrived," said Ben. "And that he can remember where the attack happened."

"I hope he doesn't think it's strange we want to know," Zoe answered. "We have to be careful what we ask, remember."

Ben grinned. "Actually I was planning to say, 'Hi, we work for Wild, which is a top secret organization that we mustn't tell you about, and we're off on an undercover mission to—'"

Zoe pushed him into a pile of soft snow that had been cleared from the path. Then she scooted off, giggling, to avoid a volley of snowballs from her brother.

She almost collided with a young man in a bright red snow jacket who was making his way down the path. One of Ben's snowballs hit him on the chest.

Ben ran up, looking sheepish.

"I'm so sorry!" he panted, as the young man brushed off the snow. "I was aiming at my sister."

"No problem!" The man grinned. He had a round, cheerful face, with brown skin and a shock of black hair under his hood. "I heard there were two kids out here who wanted to know about my encounter with the bear. I guess I've found you – or rather, you've found me! Lukie's the name."

"I'm Zoe and this is Ben," said Zoe eagerly. "We read about you on Mr Airut's blog before we came away on holiday. We'd be very interested to hear about your encounter with the polar bear."

"If I had a dollar for every time I've been asked to tell this story, I'd be a rich man," said Lukie, eyes twinkling. "I could give you a tale of great bravery. I could speak of how I tracked down the mighty snow beast and slew it with my bare hands. But in truth I was out ice fishing and suddenly there she was, the length of two kayaks away."

"What happened?" asked Ben, wide-eyed.

"I had to think very quickly, Ben," said Lukie. "I knew I had to let her get my scent so that she could identify me as human. Polar bears usually back off then."

"But she didn't…" prompted Zoe.

"She stared hard at me with her deep, dark eyes," Lukie went on. "And all the time she was baring her teeth and hissing."

"I've read about that sort of behaviour," said Ben. "That sounds like one angry bear."

"I'll never forget it, that's for sure," said Lukie. "I stood tall and waved my arms to scare her, but it didn't work. She began to move towards me and the next thing she was lowering her head and … CHARGING!"

He roared, making Ben and Zoe jump.

They grinned at each other, a little embarrassed.

"I knew I'd never outrun her," Lukie went on. "There was only one thing I could do. I fumbled for my gun and for a second I thought I was too late. But somehow I managed to get a shot off just as she reared up for the final attack."

"The blog we read said she was a lactating mother," said Zoe. "Wasn't that unusual? I mean, for a mother to leave her cubs?"

Lukie thought for a moment. "I guess so," he replied. "I remember Theo said she was very thin. She must have been desperate for food."

"So she saw you as a meal," said Ben.

Lukie nodded. "I was sorry to kill her, but it was either her or me."

"Did you see any cubs?" Zoe asked anxiously.

"I can see you're an animal lover, Zoe," said the fisherman. "There was no sign of any cubs. I didn't know then that she was a mother, and I didn't stick around in case there were any more ravenous bears about. I got the carcass back by towing it behind my kayak. I couldn't just leave it there. The Inupiat are allowed to kill polar bears, but according to our law the carcass must be registered with the Fish and Wildlife Service. And we are not allowed to waste a kill. Anyway, Theo heard about it and wanted to have a look first. It was only when he made his examination that I found out she must have had cubs somewhere." He sighed. "We don't hunt mother bears. We want to keep bear numbers up."

"Is there a map where you could show us the place it happened?" asked Ben. "You should put a flag or something on there to mark your brave encounter."

"Follow me," said Lukie, with a smile. He led them over to one of the maps they had seen outside the entrance to the centre. "This is our latest update of the extent of the ice cover in this area," he explained. "And I was here."

To Ben and Zoe's surprise, Lukie did not point to anywhere on the land. Instead his

finger went straight to the north side of a
large island of ice, separated from Fairwood
by a wide channel of water. "I must have
been about here on this floe," he said.
"That spur that sticks out to the north.
I always find a good supply of cod there."

"But that's just floating ice!" exclaimed
Ben, shocked. "I thought bears built
birthing dens on the mainland. What was
she doing out there?"

"A few bears make their dens in the snow
banks on the ice floes," said Lukie.

The saleswoman waved at him from the
door. "Lukie!" she called. "There's a delivery
of guidebooks. I need your muscles!"

Lukie gave them a rueful grin and went
off to help.

Ben peered closely at the map. He was
memorizing the coordinates of the area.
Once they were entered into their BUGs,
it would make the search much easier.

"This changes everything," he said. "We've got to reach that ice floe and there's a bit of Arctic Ocean in the way."

Zoe gazed solemnly out at the bleak stretch of icy water. "This mission's going to be much more dangerous than we thought."

CHAPTER FIVE

"This is a cool way to travel!" called Zoe, as they paddled their kayaks across the grey, choppy water, heading for the ice floe. They had their hoods up and goggles on against the cold.

"Certainly would be if you fell in!" said Ben.

As soon as the children had told Erika that they needed to get out on to the floe she'd taken action. She'd hired the kayaks from the visitors' centre with the cover story that they'd be off for two days' exploring.

Once out of sight of Fairwood, their "mother" had left them and headed off further along the coast towards the site where the proposed oil drilling would take place.

"These kayaks would be really fast if it wasn't for the ice in the water," said Zoe, skilfully steering a path through the floating

obstacles. "I'm glad we brushed up our canoeing skills during our training week."

In some places the ice lay in flat pieces looking like a shattered mirror; in others they formed natural ice sculptures which towered above them, glinting in the afternoon sunlight.

Ben slipped his BUG out of his pocket. "Good thing Uncle Stephen thought to give us these special thin gloves." He laughed. "We'd never manage to hit the right buttons if our fingers were as thick as sausages." He called up the satellite map. "We're heading in the right direction," he said. "About another twenty minutes and we'll reach the southern tip of the ice floe. Then we've got the trek across it."

"Not so much a trek – more a whiz," said Zoe. "I can't wait to try out my RAT."

"There's a problem up ahead," said Ben suddenly. "The satellite picture shows we'll be going into thick fog. It'll be hard to see and much colder."

Soon they could see a bank of white dense vapour swirling on the surface of the sea in front of them. There didn't seem to be any way around.

"Thank goodness we've got our BUGs to

guide us," said Zoe. "We'd end up going round in circles otherwise."

They paddled into the thick fog. It was impossible to see much further than the end of the kayak.

"Stay close to me," called Ben urgently.

Following the northwards course on their BUGs, they made their way blindly through the thick, freezing air. The paddling movement was keeping them warm, but they could feel droplets of ice clinging to their hoods and balaclavas. The only noise was the splash of their oars and the occasional clunking sound as ice blocks clashed together.

"I'll be glad to reach the floe," said Zoe. She was paddling as close as she could to Ben's side to keep him in sight.

"Me too," answered Ben. "This is creepy."

Something dark loomed up in the fog. The children slowed their kayaks.

"What's that?" Zoe whimpered. "It looks like a row of grey people in hoods … and they're crouched down. I don't like it."

Now they could hear sounds as if someone was tapping on wood. Zoe back-paddled as fast as she could.

"Surely it can't be humans," said Ben, trying to sound braver than he felt.

He tapped a key on his BUG to identify the sound. When the result flashed up on the screen he burst out laughing with relief.

"Come back," he called to his sister. "It's just a pod of walruses. It was their shapes you could see – they're on the ice floe."

The fog swirled and cleared a little, and in the small shaft of sunlight they could see the walruses lying on the edge of the ice. Their pinky-grey bodies were covered in short hair and their snouts bristled with stiff whiskers. Each one had a pair of gleaming tusks, pointing downwards and looking very sharp.

With a shamefaced grin, Zoe brought her kayak alongside his again. "Well, they looked scary back there," she insisted.

"We don't want to land amongst them," said Ben. "I know they don't usually attack humans, but they're huge."

"And those tusks look vicious," agreed Zoe. "I vote we give them a wide berth."

One of the walruses was watching them with its little eyes, turning its head to follow their movements. It raised its snout to the air, whiskers twitching. Suddenly it gave a harsh, bellowing cry. The other animals took it up and they began to shuffle towards the sea.

"They've caught our scent and they're scared," said Ben, plunging his paddle into the water. "We should have used the scent dispersers on our BUGs, but it's too late now. Get away as fast as you can. Walruses always take to the sea when they're frightened."

Just as he spoke, the walruses plunged
into the icy ocean with tremendous
splashes. Waves of water surged towards the
kayaks. Ben and Zoe rowed madly back into
the fog, but more animals were diving into
the sea. Shiny heads were popping up all
over the place, giving terrified cries as they
swam away.

Zoe let out a yelp of fright as the wash of
water tipped her sideways. Ben twisted in his
seat to try and spot his sister through the
wall of fog. But Zoe was nowhere to be seen.

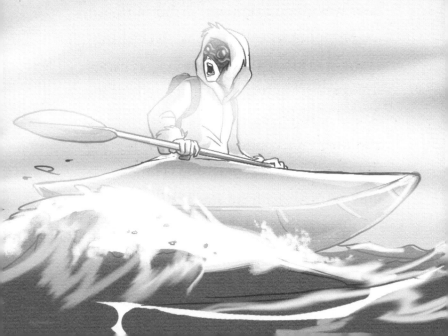

CHAPTER SIX

"Zoe!" Ben's voice sounded muffled in the fog. "Zoe, where are you?"

He listened. For a moment all he could hear was the crunch and grind of floating ice bumping into the kayak. His heart raced. He knew that if Zoe had capsized she couldn't survive long in the freezing Arctic water.

He began to paddle around, searching the choppy waves. Nothing. Hands shaking with fear, he steered the kayak through the ice, looking to right and left.

He called again. This time he could hear the rising panic in his own voice. Vital minutes were passing.

Then at last he heard a call, so faint at first that he thought he was imagining what he wanted to hear. No, there it was again. He propelled the kayak quickly towards the sound through the swirling fog.

"Ben!" Now he could see the outline of a figure on the edge of the ice floe. It was waving frantically.

He swiftly brought his kayak up to the bank of ice. Zoe was kneeling, her hand stretched towards him to help him climb out.

"I thought you'd capsized!" panted Ben, as he pulled his lightweight craft out of the water and put it next to his sister's.

"I nearly did!" Zoe replied. "I was so scared. The walruses made such rough waves! Remember that capsize session we did with Erika in the canoes?"

Ben nodded. "You were really good at it."

"Just as well," said Zoe. "Every time I felt myself keeling over I just about managed to slap the water with the paddle and twist myself up. As soon as the walruses had gone I got myself on to the ice. I never want to do that again."

Ben could hear a tremble in her voice. "Well, we're both OK," he said, putting his arm round her shoulders. "But we must be more careful."

"Too right," said Zoe, vehemently. "Let's get away from here."

"Mustn't forget to fit our trackers to the kayaks first," said Ben. "Then we'll be able to locate them wherever we are."

He detached a small gadget from his BUG and clipped it firmly on to the kayak. Zoe did the same with hers. They then turned them upside down and covered them with snow.

"We don't want anyone passing to see empty kayaks and try to rescue us," said Zoe.

Ben checked the screen of his BUG. An orange light pulsed. "Tracker's working."

He tapped some more keys. "I've put in the coordinates I remembered from the map Lukie showed us," he told Zoe. He studied the map on his screen and pointed across the snow. "It's this way. Northward ho!"

BUG SAT MAP
KEY
= SNOW RIDGES
N
ARCTIC OCEAN
FAIRWOOD
MAIN STREET
INUPIAT HERITAGE CENTER

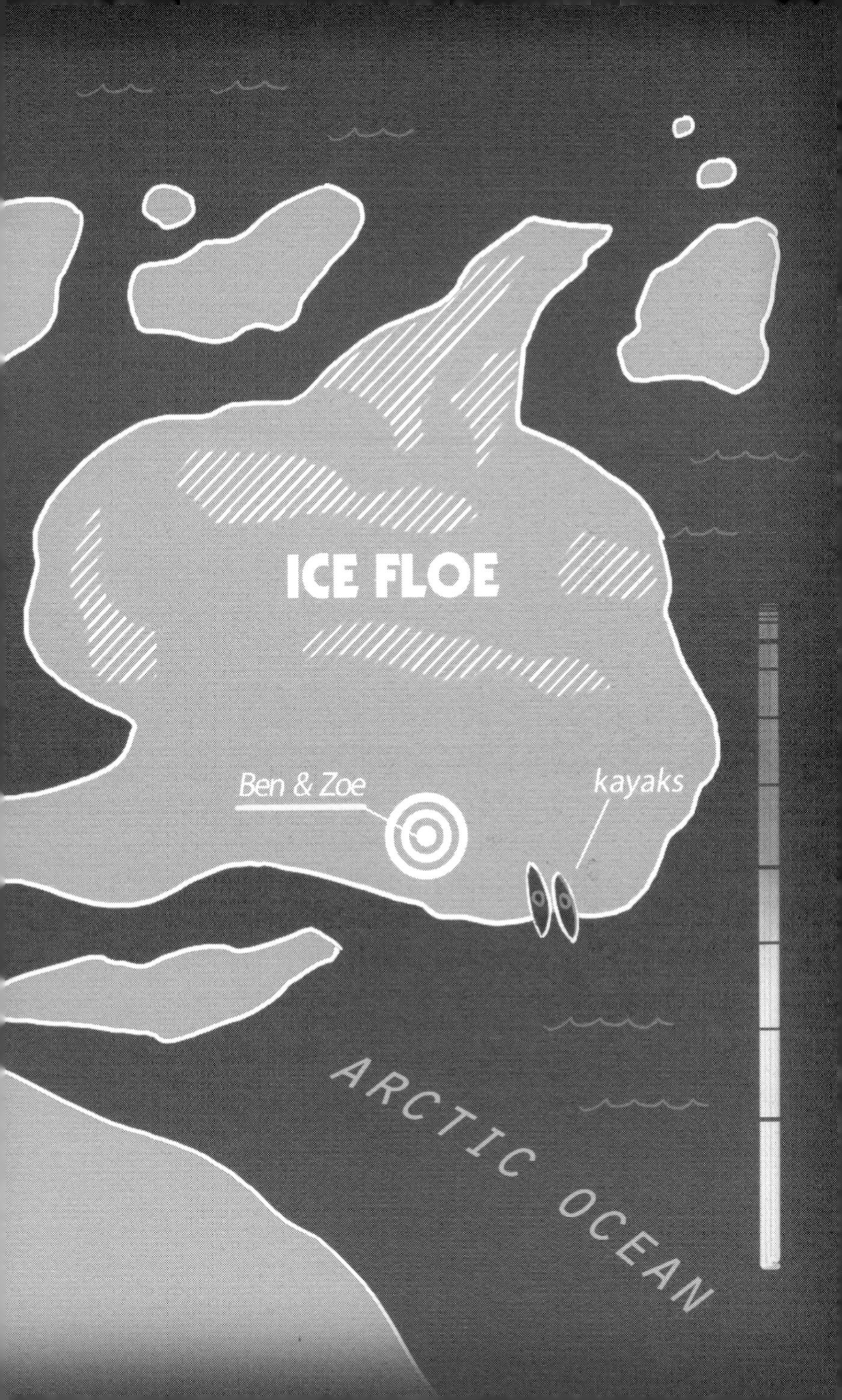

ICE FLOE
Ben & Zoe
kayaks
ARCTIC OCEAN

"And now – time for the RATs," declared Zoe. The two children pulled their slim snowboards out of the side pockets of their backpacks and put them down on the snow.

They looked out towards their destination. At their feet the ice floe was covered in a smooth, flat layer of snow, but further on the ice had been sculpted into strange shapes by the wind. Some formations made gentle mounds; others looked like sheer jagged rocks, their ledges thick with overhanging snow.

The children pressed their heels on to the starting buttons and the RATs' motors whizzed into life. Off they went, weaving two parallel tracks in the untrodden snow. Ben surged ahead.

"Watch this!" he yelled back to his sister. He steered the RAT towards a hump in the ground and took off, balancing expertly in the air with outstretched arms.

"Olympic jump!" he boasted, as he landed several metres further on.

A look of grim determination on her face, Zoe copied him. She glanced back at the two landing marks in the snow and grinned. Her jump was longer.

"You only got the silver medal," she called. "I got the gold!"

She put on a burst of speed and zoomed after her brother. Ben slowed a little, then, checking she was close behind, stamped down with his heel on the back of his RAT. The end dug into the snow and a powdery white spray flew up behind it – all over Zoe.

Ben burst out laughing and zoomed away, Zoe on his tail. But suddenly he brought his RAT to a halt. Zoe just managed to avoid colliding with him.

"A joke's a joke," she said crossly, "but I nearly ran into you then."

"Sorry," said Ben. "But check out that sky ahead."

Zoe stared at the horizon. Grey clouds were swirling round in the distance. They were getting closer and the wind was whipping the snow around their feet.

"That's bad," Zoe said simply. "Looks like a snowstorm. Remember the old man at the centre said there was one coming. That's going to delay us getting to the cubs."

The low sun was now completely blotted out by the dark, ominous clouds. Flakes of snow were falling fast. They were being driven straight into their faces by the wind. Ben and Zoe couldn't keep their balance on the RATs and had to walk instead.

"I can't see a thing," yelled Zoe, as they trudged along. "And it's getting much colder. I'm not sure how much further I can go."

"This is hopeless," said Ben. "Let's get the tent up. We'd be better sitting out the storm than getting lost – or worse."

He reached into his backpack and pulled out the compactly folded tent. Together they tried to open it up, but the buffeting wind kept pulling at it, threatening to pull it from their grasp. The thin material was slipping through their gloved hands like a wet fish.

"Don't let go!" yelled Ben.

But it was too late. There was a vicious blast of wind and the tent was torn out of their hands. It whipped away until it was a tiny dot on the horizon.

CHAPTER SEVEN

"Now what are we going to do?" asked Ben desperately. "We'll never survive out here in a snowstorm."

"We have to take shelter," said Zoe. "Remember what Amaguq said about snow holes? We need to make one – now!"

"The ground looks raised over there." Ben pointed into the distance. "There might be enough snow to dig into."

"It's hard to see anything!" shouted Zoe, struggling to walk against the rising strength of the wind, which howled around them and tugged at their clothes.

At last they reached the banked-up snow and dropped to their knees, the wind blasting into their faces.

"Perfect!" yelled Ben. "It's facing away from the wind!"

"I wish *we* were!" Zoe yelled back.

They clawed blindly at the snow.

"It's falling too fast to clear!" called Ben.

"Use your RAT as a spade!" The children were soon scooping great shovelfuls of snow away with the front end of the boards.

At last they'd scooped out a space just big enough to crawl into. They took off their goggles and lay huddled together in their sleeping bags, listening to the wind roaring outside. Zoe pulled a torch out of her backpack. She shone its beam at the entrance to their shelter. It lit the snowflakes that were driving past the entrance. The storm was at its height.

"It's unbelievable," said Ben. "We've seen snowstorms like this on television, but I never realized how bad it would be to land up in the middle of one."

"It's going to delay our search," said Zoe. "Those poor cubs."

"It could go on for hours." Ben sighed. "We'll have to make the best of it. How about some provisions? I'm hungry."

"You're always hungry," laughed Zoe, wriggling round to put her hand into her brother's backpack. "If you get your elbow out of my stomach, I might be able to reach the food."

"Not easy!" Ben shifted painfully. "Now I'm sitting on the RAT's motor."

The children soon had their high-energy fruit bars unwrapped. They sat and munched in silence. Outside it was as dark as night now, and the snow was piling up at the hole's entrance. Strange noises rose up above the whine of the wind.

"That's the ice floe creaking," said Zoe.
"It moves all the time and this storm's
making it worse." She scooped some snow
into her glove and sucked at it. "No
shortage of drink here."

Ben yawned and rubbed his eyes. "I'm going to get a bit of sleep," he told Zoe. "Jet lag. Wake me up when the storm's over."

Zoe nodded. Ben always suffered more than she did from the time changes when they went on their missions. She knew she wouldn't sleep anyway. Her mind was too busy picturing the shivering bear cubs alone in their den. She wondered how they'd ever get to them in time. Any tracks the mother polar bear or fisherman had left would be covered in fresh snow. So would the den…

Zoe's breathing was quickening and her thoughts were suddenly tumbling about. She had a weird feeling of confusion. She turned to Ben and was horrified to see that his lips were blue – and yet when she touched his skin it was warm. What was happening?

She shook her brother hard. She was relieved to see he was breathing, but he wouldn't stir. Her muddled brain tried to work out what was going on. She had to get a grip on herself, but she felt so light-headed! She took a handful of snow and rubbed it in her face to wake herself up.

She flashed the torch around. Where was the entrance to their shelter? It had vanished. Was she having a nightmare? No, that was silly, she was awake.

And now the tiny bit of Zoe's brain that was still working had the answer. The storm had sealed them in. They were trapped in a tomb of snow. If the hole had gone, then no air was getting in. They were being starved of oxygen. That explained why she felt so strange. And that was why Ben wouldn't wake up.

Zoe knew that if she didn't do something straight away they were going to die! But all she wanted to do was close her eyes and sleep.

"Stay awake!" she muttered to herself,
pinching her cheeks hard, hoping the pain
would keep her focused.

She started to scrape at the covered
entrance, but the snow was thick and she
could feel her strength draining away. She
was gasping now from lack of air as she
clawed desperately for a way out.

Then, just when she thought she couldn't dig any more, the snow fell away and her gloved hand broke through the wall. With the last of her strength, Zoe heaved herself up to the small gap and took great welcome gulps of freezing air. She felt her brain slowly come back to life. She twisted round to Ben.

He was pale and still. Zoe's heart almost stopped. Was she too late?

CHAPTER EIGHT

"Wake up, Ben!" Zoe tugged at her brother's jacket and managed to haul him towards the small blast of fresh, freezing air. His head lolled forwards and he didn't stir.

"Ben!" sobbed Zoe in desperation. She rubbed hard on his back. Then she shook him. But nothing was working.

Desperately she took a handful of snow and shoved it into his face.

Ben gave a faint groan and his eyelids fluttered. "Gerroff!" he mumbled.

Zoe didn't think she'd ever been happier!

She got another handful of snow.

"Cold!" muttered Ben, trying to turn his head away.

"Breathe deeply," insisted Zoe, slapping his cheeks. "You lost consciousness."

Gradually, Ben came round. To Zoe's relief his skin began to look pinker, although his eyes were still heavy and he slumped back against the wall of the snow hole. She thrust an energy bar into his hand and watched him slowly chew it.

"What happened?" Ben said groggily.

"Our entrance got covered over with snow and we'd forgotten to make an air hole," answered Zoe. "Amaguq said it was really important."

"I bet polar bears remember to do that when they build a den." Ben grinned weakly.

"We must start searching for the cubs' den as soon as you feel ready," said Zoe. "I can't hear the wind any more."

Ben dug at the entrance until it was wide enough for him to see through. "It's dark out there!" he said. "We must have been here hours."

Zoe checked her BUG. "It's eight in the evening."

"It's stopped snowing," Ben reported. "Let's go."

They pulled their goggles back on, broke out of their shelter and stood in the dark landscape. The snow clouds had gone as quickly as they'd come. A pale moon shone, making the sky an inky blue. The children switched on small flashlights that were stitched into the front of their balaclavas.

"Visibility OK," grinned Ben. A light flashed on his BUG screen. "We're close to where the attack happened," he said. "The den shouldn't be too far away." He pressed a key and an arrow flashed on the screen. "Follow me."

The children jumped on to their RATs and sped off across the new, powdery snow, stopping every now and then to check the direction.

"It looks like the ground's moving up ahead," said Zoe at last, slowing down her RAT.

Ben peered forwards. "That's the sea," he exclaimed. "It's the floating ice that you can see moving. Good old BUG, it hasn't let us down. We're on the spur."

"It's a lot wider than I expected," said Zoe looking around. "I can't see the water on the other side."

They jumped off their boards, folded them and put them back in their backpacks. Ben tapped some keys. "I've set it to look for the thickest snow banks," he said. "That's sure to be where the den is."

"Time for thermal imaging." Zoe pressed the logo at the side of her snow goggles.

At once the bottom half of the lenses became cloudy. As she looked at Ben, she could see his top half clearly but his legs showed up as a purple, yellow and orange glow. "With luck we'll pick up the cubs' body heat."

If they're still alive, she thought to herself.

"There's a long ridge of snow twenty metres along the spur from here," said Ben, clicking his goggles into thermal mode as well. "Let's start our search there."

Reaching the ridge, they moved slowly along, staring intently through the bottom half of their goggles, but there was no sign of the glowing shape of a warm, living body.

"They're not here," said Ben as they reached the end. He tapped at one key and then another on his BUG. "That's strange. I can't seem to update this map. The screen seems to have stuck."

"Mine's stuck too," said Zoe in surprise.

"Do you think it's too cold for them?" She pressed the hot key that would put them in touch with Wild Headquarters. "I'll ask Uncle Stephen." She gave the BUG a shake. "No, that's not working either. This is scary, Ben. How will we find our kayaks again or contact HQ?"

"It's strange," said Ben. "Surely Uncle Stephen would have adapted our BUGs for these conditions. We'll just have to carry on our search the hard way and worry about the rest later." He scanned the snowy ground as far as his light shone for likely den sites.

"The blizzard hasn't helped things," said Zoe. "The snow's covered any tracks."

"Let's look for another ridge," suggested Ben. "The den has to be somewhere on this spur of ice."

They trudged across the snow until a high bank came into view.

"Look!" gasped Zoe, pointing at a small
hole. "Can you see it? My goggles have
picked up something living in there."

"The image is about the right size for a
cub," said Ben in excitement.

"Wait," Zoe warned him. "That's not a
very big entrance. I don't think a polar bear
would fit…"

Too late. Ben had stuck his hand in.

There was a snarl and he leaped back. "Yow!" he gasped. "I nearly got bitten."

A small white snout appeared at the opening. Sharp teeth and bright eyes gleamed in their lamps.

"It's an Arctic fox," said Zoe, as the terrified animal shot into the darkness. "This is hopeless." She sighed. "How are we going to find the ridges to search without our BUGs?"

"Let's be methodical," said Ben. "We can
see where we've been from our footprints.
Let's keep the moon behind us and move
forwards up the spur. But it's going to take
a while."

They seemed to trudge for ages,
getting colder by the minute. No
matter where they looked, nothing
showed on their thermogoggles.

Zoe stopped to stamp her feet
and clap her hands to warm
herself. "Why is there a purple
glow ahead on the horizon?"
she called to Ben. "It can't
possibly be dawn – that's the
wrong direction."

Before their astonished
eyes, the glow grew brighter
and an arc of vivid green
light streaked across the sky.

CHAPTER NINE

Ben and Zoe watched, mesmerized, as long shimmering curtains of light wove their way through the dark sky. The colours swirled and flashed above their heads.

Zoe clutched Ben's arm. "What's happening?" she breathed. "It's so weird!"

To her surprise he was grinning from ear to ear. "Don't be scared. It's the aurora borealis."

"The northern lights!" cried Zoe. "Of course! This is awesome! I've always wanted to see them – but I never thought they'd be like this."

They gazed up as luminous yellow ribbons danced across the sky, followed by waving beams of red and green. At times the children could almost see giant faces and shapes in the billowing colours.

"Now I can see why there are stories about them being gods in the sky," murmured Zoe.

"They're actually caused by particles from the sun colliding with the oxygen and nitrogen atoms in the atmosphere," Ben told her.

"Thanks, Mr Walking Encyclopaedia," joked Zoe. Then she caught her breath. "I think I know why our BUGs stopped working," she said thoughtfully. "It must be all this electrical activity." She scanned the area. "But look how well it's lighting up the terrain."

"You're right," said Ben, pointing eagerly. "I didn't see that tall bank of snow ahead."

Zoe nodded. "Could be the very place for a polar bear den."

They jumped on to their RATs and set off for the snow bank, which shimmered with the reflected glow from above.

"Thank you, northern lights," Zoe yelled up at the sky. "We can see really well now. It could be day. Sorry we haven't got time to watch the whole show."

They skidded to a stop where the bank began, sending up a shower of snow.

"It's much bigger than I thought," said Ben. He looked up and down the long ridge through his thermogoggles. "It'll take hours to search this lot."

"Got an idea," said Zoe. "If it's the weird electricity of the aurora borealis that's interfering with the BUGs then it might only be their satellite function that's affected." She held her BUG out in triumph. "I was right," she said. "Look, the scent disperser's OK and the animal cry analysis."

"Great, then we can set that to pick up the cubs' call," said Ben. "It has a much wider range than the thermogoggles."

"The lights are getting fainter," said Zoe, looking up to see a fading red glow in the distance. "It'll be dark again soon. We must search as quickly as we can while there's still some extra light."

They moved along the bank, scanning every centimetre of snow with the goggles and checking their BUGs for an indication that the cubs were nearby. But the glow in the sky was fast disappearing, and soon they were relying on their headlamps and the pale moonlight to find their way.

Zoe stopped and held up her BUG. It was flashing. "Polar bear cub cry," she read excitedly.

"Where's it coming from?" said Ben.

"That's strange," said Zoe, frowning. "It can't be coming from a den. The cry's well away from the bank." She spun round and pointed at a jagged point of ice that rose up from the snow. "Behind there, I think."

Ben set off quickly, his boots sending up sprays of snow as he ran.

"Slow down," warned Zoe. "You don't want to scare it."

As they rounded the point of ice, Zoe saw something in the beam from her headlamp.

It was a tiny bear cub.

CHAPTER TEN

The little white bundle of fur lay curled up
in the snow.

"The poor little thing," gasped Zoe. "It
must be one of our orphans. It's left the den
looking for its mum."

"Is it still alive?" asked Ben anxiously.

Zoe peered closely. "I can see its chest
moving," she said with relief.

She quickly pulled the fleecy sling out of
her backpack. "Help me get it in, Ben." She
bent over the cub. "We've got to warm you
up, haven't we," she told it in a gooey voice.

"You'd be better off growling at it," said
Ben, unfolding the sling. "We've got to be
like its mum, remember."

Zoe lifted the little cub up. As Uncle
Stephen had said, it was about the size of a
large cat, with dark eyes that blinked at
Zoe. "It's a girl," she said. She laid the cub
on to the fleece and gently wrapped it
around her. The cub gave a small mewing
sound and nuzzled into the fur.

Ben helped Zoe fix the sling on so that
the bear was secure
against her chest.
All of a sudden,
Zoe felt something
tug at her glove.

The little cub
was sucking
noisily at the
end of one of
the fingers.

"We'll get you some food as soon as we can," she said. "But first we're going to check your den to see if you've got any brothers or sisters."

"Pass me your BUG," said Ben. "I'll set it to give off a female polar bear scent so that Junior here thinks you're her mum."

Zoe handed it over and as she did so, she caught sight of something in the snow. Tiny prints with five claws were clearly visible, leading away across the snow towards the far end of the bank. "Look, here are her tracks," she said. "The long ones are the front paws. Five pads and claws on each. She must have come out after the storm."

They started to follow the trail. The prints led towards the ridge in a wobbly line.

The little cub began to wriggle and grunt. "I think she's warming up," said Zoe. "And that's made her realize she's hungry. We'll have to feed her soon."

After a few minutes they
came across a dip in the bank.
Looking through the thermal part
of their goggles, they could see a faint
orangey-purple glow, deep inside the snow.

"I think we've found another one!"
exclaimed Zoe.

"There's a tunnel here," said Ben,
brushing away the snow. "I'm going to
explore."

"Don't get stuck," said Zoe.

"No chance," grinned Ben. "It must be wide enough for a polar bear, remember. They're a lot fatter than me."

He got down on his belly and shuffled into the hole until Zoe could only see the soles of his boots. Then his feet disappeared inside. Zoe watched anxiously at the entrance. Eventually, Ben's beaming face appeared.

"Got it," he cried. "It's very weak, but it still tried to bite me just like the fox." He examined his glove. "Good old Uncle Stephen. Not only are these gloves ultra-thin, they're fang-proof as well."

He began to go back down the tunnel, feet first. "It's warmer in here than out there," he called. "Just the place for feeding time."

Zoe crawled quickly after him. There was room for her to go on her hands and knees so she didn't have to undo the sling. The tunnel gave way to a small chamber.

Ben was putting the new cub into its
fleece.

"It's another girl," he told Zoe. "She's
smaller than her sister and not as strong."

"But we've got them!" squealed Zoe in
delight. "I was beginning to think this was
one Wild mission that was going to be
impossible."

"It's not over till we've got them back,"
replied Ben.

"And they'll need food before we set off,"
said his sister. She unpacked the bottles and
dried milk. Stuffing snow into a bottle, she
melted it with a small battery-operated
element.

When it was warm, she added a
portion of dried milk. The cubs got the
scent and began to squeal and wriggle.
Zoe quickly attached teats and handed one
of the bottles to Ben.

"Better give it to them slowly," she

warned, as her cub sucked frantically.
"It will be a shock to their empty tummies."

"I'm going to call this one Guzzle," said
Ben, as he tried to release the teat from his
cub's mouth. "She slurps every time she
sucks. She may be small and weak, but she's
determined to survive."

"My one won't stop poking its nose into
everything I do," said Zoe, scratching her
furry head. "Nosy is the name for you."

She looked around the den. The walls were smooth with a claw mark here and there where the mother had dug. "This is quite roomy," said Zoe.

"Luxury accommodation," grinned Ben, "compared to our little snow hole anyway."

As soon as the cubs had finished, Zoe crawled along the tunnel, shivering as the freezing outside air hit her face. "Time for the homeward journey," she said.

Standing outside the den, she checked the satellite function on her BUG. "Hey!" she called to Ben as he emerged. "It's working properly now. We'll be able to find our way back to the kayaks using the trackers."

"I reckon your theory about the interference was right," said Ben. "Now the northern lights have gone everything's fine."

Zoe stepped on to her RAT. "Shame in

a way," she sighed. "It was such a fantastic show."

Checking that their charges were comfortable, the children set off on their snowboards back along the spur of ice towards the main floe.

"It's a lot harder to balance with a polar bear cub on board!" Zoe shouted to her brother, as she sped along in front of him.

Ben didn't reply. She turned to see what the matter was. Her brother had stopped way back and was looking around.

"I can hear a boat," he called.

Zoe could hear it too. The deep throbbing hum of an engine. Then she saw it in the distance. It was a cruise ship, casting out a glow of golden light from every window, and it seemed to be heading very close to the floe. Behind thick glass windows, they could see people dancing at a late night party.

"Hide!" she yelled, ducking down behind the ridge. "We mustn't be seen." She quickly turned off her headlamp. Ben found a jagged ice formation and squatted in its shadow.

The throbbing noise grew louder and the ice beneath them began to vibrate.

Just how close is this ship going to come? thought Ben. *If it ploughs through the ice we don't stand a chance.*

Now the ship towered above them, gliding slowly past the ice floe. The rumbling of its engines was deafening and the children could feel it shaking their bodies. The cubs whimpered in fear.

There was a terrible crash and a fierce judder ran along the ice!

"It's hit the end of the spur," yelled Zoe.

A dark jagged line zigzagged over the snow in front of Ben. The spur of ice was breaking away from the main floe, leaving Zoe on one side and him on the other.

Ben was stranded.

CHAPTER ELEVEN

Ben and Zoe stared horrified at the widening channel of freezing Arctic water between them. The ship carried smoothly on past.

"Stay there," shouted Zoe. "I'll go and fetch a kayak."

"No," Ben shouted back. "By the time you get back I could have drifted miles away. Don't worry. I've got a plan."

"You're not to do anything stupid," called Zoe.

Ben didn't reply. Instead he turned his

RAT and steered away from the broken edge of the spur.

"Where are you going?" cried Zoe in alarm.

"Stand back," Ben shouted. He brought the RAT to a halt and swivelled it round in the snow. Now he was facing Zoe again. With a look of grim determination on his face he revved up the motor. Then he set off, accelerating until he was racing along at top speed towards the water.

With a stab of horror, Zoe suddenly realized what her daredevil brother was about to do. He was going to jump the gap.

"No!" she shrieked. "You'll never make it!"

But she knew it was too late. Ben was already crouching on his board, both arms stretched out for balance. She hardly dared watch as he sprang up into the air towards her, the whirring RAT at his feet. It was a huge jump – and made even more difficult with the weight of the cub in its sling. And every second the channel of deadly water was widening. For a moment it looked as if Ben was going to plunge straight into the freezing depths.

Now he was almost at the bank – but surely he couldn't make it! Zoe let out a scream as her brother landed on the very edge of the ice. A loud cracking noise ripped through the air as the ice began to fall away into the water.

Desperately, Ben waved his arms to get his balance, then flung himself forwards. Boy, cub and RAT toppled on to the ice. But they were safe. Zoe darted over to him. Ben got to his knees, checked he hadn't squashed Guzzle and raised his hand for a high five.

"OK," said his sister, pulling him to his feet. "You get the Olympic gold this time."

"It was nothing." Ben grinned. "You can have my autograph later."

Ben wasn't going to admit that he'd felt as scared as Zoe looked. It had been a big risk, and he didn't like to think of what would have happened if he hadn't made it.

Ben stroked Guzzle's head, and the little cub popped her head up. She began to wriggle about, trying to get out of the sling.

"I don't blame you, Guzzle!" said Ben. "That was a bit of a hairy moment."

The children checked the kayak tracker and whizzed off across the ice floe, their headlamps lighting the way as they went. The storm had blown the snow into frozen ripples. There were occasional animal tracks trailing across it. Zoe cut a figure of eight and came up alongside Ben, spraying up an arc of powdery snow.

"Couldn't resist," she called. "If we got snow like this at home, we'd be out all day making snowmen and having snowball fights and sledging... What's the matter?" Ben was frowning.

"I'm a bit worried about Guzzle," he said.

"Doesn't she look good?" asked Zoe.

"Just the opposite," groaned Ben. "She wants to get out. Her wriggling's putting me off balance!"

"Not long now." Zoe laughed. "Look, there are our kayaks. We'll soon get her to someone who can look after her." In the moonlight, the snowy outlines were just visible in the distance.

"Top speed then," yelled Ben.

But Zoe had stopped. "There's something further along the edge of the floe." She pointed to a large, dark shape in the snow.

"Nothing to worry about," called Ben. "It's just a lump of ice, isn't it?"

Zoe gulped. "Lumps of ice can't walk," she said slowly. "It's coming towards us, Ben. It's a polar bear."

"You're right," said Ben fearfully. He brought his RAT to a halt. "Wave your arms and make yourself as tall as possible. We mustn't look scared."

Zoe did as he said although she could feel her heart thumping with fright. The huge polar bear raised its head to the sky and gave a ferocious growl.

"Hope it's not hungry," she whispered.

"We must show it we're human – and

dominant," Ben told her quickly. "Go
away!" he yelled in his deepest voice.
Zoe joined in. But the bear began to pad
towards them.

"It's not working," said Zoe, trying to keep the wobble out of her voice as the bear picked up speed.

Now it was galloping towards them, strong legs pounding away at the snow, sharp teeth gleaming. It was covering the gap between them quickly – too quickly.

It wasn't only the cubs that needed saving now.

CHAPTER TWELVE

All at once Zoe's brain clicked into gear. She had a mad notion but it just might work.

"Go!" she yelled to Ben. "Use your RAT and escape!" She turned so that her board was facing away from their advancing attacker.

"Even on these we can't go faster than a bear," cried Ben desperately.

"Trust me!" she screamed. "I'll be right behind, I promise."

Ben knew better than to argue. "You'd better be." He jumped on his RAT, clutched

Guzzle tightly to stop her moving, and sped away.

Trying to keep calm, Zoe kicked her RAT into action. The bear was almost upon her. It reared up, massive front paws raised ready to crush her. Zoe tipped the back of the RAT into the snow and revved hard just as Ben had done earlier when he'd given her an icy shower. At once the motor caught on the soft snow and sent up a thick spray straight into the face of the bear. With a frightened growl it recoiled.

Zoe didn't waste a second. She moved her weight forwards and chased after her brother. Every now and then she shifted her back foot to keep up the thick mist. When she dared to peek over her shoulder, she couldn't see the bear. The air was thick with flying snow.

She caught up with Ben and they made a wide arc round towards the kayaks. After a few minutes, Zoe glanced back again. There was no sign of the bear.

"I think it's given up," she called to her brother.

He stopped and scanned the route they'd taken. "Can't see or hear it," he said in relief. "Well done, Zoe. I thought we were bear breakfast! Let's get out of here quickly in case it decides to come back."

They dug their kayaks out of the snow and got into them right on the edge of the ice. Then they pushed off and launched themselves with a splash on to the icy water.

When they had paddled a good distance away from the ice, Ben called up the satellite map.

"I don't need that to tell me which way to go," said Zoe. She pointed over to where the sky was shot with the pinky glow of dawn. "That's got to be east and we want south."

"You're such an expert." Ben grinned. "The Inupiat people will be begging you to stay."

Zoe stuck out her tongue at him. Then she checked her little charge and laughed. "Nosy has no idea what we've been through for her," she said. "She's fast asleep."

"So's Guzzle," replied Ben. "At last!"

"Let's find out where to take them," said Zoe, hitting the hot key on her BUG for Wild HQ.

"Hello there!" Uncle Stephen's eager voice boomed out. "What's been happening?"

"We've found two cubs," Zoe told him. "And we're heading back to the mainland now."

"Good show!" cried their godfather happily. "There's a polar bear rehabilitation centre a few miles down the coast from Fairwood."

Zoe's BUG vibrated and a set of coordinates flashed on to the screen.

"That's where it is," said Uncle Stephen. "It's called the Puyuk Shelter. It's a wonderful place and has great success with orphans, I'm told. They get the bears back into the wild without making them dependent on humans. You can take your little charges there."

"What's our cover story?" asked Zoe. "We can't tell them the truth."

"Hmmm." She could picture her godfather rubbing his chin as he thought about this. "I believe it's time for the 'leaving on the doorstep' scenario. Put the cubs by the entrance, ring the bell and run like billy-o!"

CHAPTER THIRTEEN

A bright morning sun was shining on the
Arctic ocean as Ben and Zoe walked along
the beach back to Fairwood. As soon as
they'd made sure that the cubs were safely
in the Puyuk shelter they'd sneaked back
to their kayaks and paddled away out of
sight. Erika was on her way now and was
going to meet them in the village.

"Hi there, kids!" came a familiar voice.
"You're up early!"

It was Lukie, dragging his kayak down
the beach to the water. The children

ran over to him.

"I see you've got your backpacks," said Lukie eagerly. "Going off on an adventure?"

"Well..." said Zoe.

"Just being here is an adventure!" Ben said quickly. "It's a fantastic place. I wish we had longer, but our mother will be whisking us off any minute."

"Where are you going next?" asked the fisherman.

Ben looked blank so Zoe jumped in. "Mum likes to surprise us," she said with a smile. "It's a sort of mystery tour." She glanced at the gear in his boat. "Are you going fishing?"

"I am," said Lukie. "I'm really glad I didn't risk it yesterday. That was one hell of a storm that came over. Did you hear it?"

"We certainly did!" said Ben, giving Zoe a quick glance.

"You wouldn't have wanted to be out in it, I can tell you!" declared the fisherman. "Very dangerous. But today's perfect for fishing." He jerked a thumb towards the road that led down to the water. "I think your taxi's here."

Ben and Zoe looked round. A dog sledge was gliding along the road towards them,

driven by Charlie. Erika was waving at
them from the back.

"Have a good trip!" said Lukie.

"And you," replied Zoe.

"Hope you don't meet any more bears,"
added Ben.

"So do I!" laughed Lukie, as the children
ran off towards their taxi.

Later that day, back at Wild HQ, Ben and Zoe watched anxiously with Erika as Uncle Stephen called up the Puyuk Shelter website.

They were wasting no time in checking on the progress of the cubs.

"I won't ever forget that moment," said Zoe as the site loaded. "When we put the cubs down and rang the bell…"

"…and then we realized they were still in their fleecy slings!" Ben went on. "We knew we couldn't leave any clues about Wild so we sprinted back over to them and took them out."

"And then Nosy started to wander away!" laughed Zoe. "And we thought we might have to head her off."

The website flashed up and their godfather clicked on the news tab.

"Astonishing find," he read, winking at the children. "Two cubs turned up on our doorstep yesterday morning. An early present from the Easter bunny?"

"Scroll down, Uncle Stephen," said Ben urgently. "I want to find out how Guzzle is."

"The cubs, which we've named Snow White and Ariel, were missing their mum, but with a bit of tender loving care, they are eating well and will soon join their new foster mother."

"Awesome," said Ben. "Guzzle was so sweet."

"And you say I'm the one who's always too soft about animals!" declared Zoe.

"You are," said Ben. "You get the gold medal every time. I'm just pleased they've found another mother for them."

"That's what we're here for," said Dr Fisher with a smile. He finished reading the article. "We have no idea who the cubs' human rescuers were. We only saw your boot tracks, but thank you whoever you are."

"And thank you from us," said Erika, giving the children a hug. "I'm very proud to have been your mother for a few days."

"Don't get soppy, Mum," laughed Zoe.

"Hey, Zoe," said Ben, turning back to the screen. "Here's an idea for a summer holiday. They do tourist visits at the centre. We can go and see Nosy and Guzzle, or should I say Snow White and Ariel."

"Yay!" cried Zoe. "I'd love to see them again."

"Even better." Ben grinned mischievously. "It says here: 'Why not swim with the bears, separated only by a thin sheet of glass?'"

"No thanks." Zoe laughed. "I never want to come that close to an adult polar bear again!"

POLAR BEAR SURVIVAL

Polar bears live in the Arctic region. They need sea ice for hunting and breeding, and migrate each year, following the movement of the ice.

No. of polar bears living in the world today ⟶ **20,000-25,000**

Regions in which polar bears can be found: Canada, Greenland, Norway, USA, Russia

Percentage of polar bears living in Canada: 60%

Life span: About 20 to 30 years in the wild - although most do not live beyond 15 to 18 years

Oldest polar bear recorded: 45 years old (in a zoo)

The polar bear is the largest land carnivore.

Male polar bears (boars) grow two to three times the size of females (sows). Boars can weigh more than 650kg and are about 2.5 to 3m long. The largest polar bear ever recorded was a male weighing 1,002kg and measuring 3.7m long.

Female polar bears breed about once every three years. The usual litter is twins, but occasionally there may be three or very rarely four. Cubs stay with their mum until they are about two and a half years old.

STATUS: VULNERABLE

The polar bear is classified as a vulnerable species on the red list of the International Union for Conservation of Nature. This means it is not currently endangered, but its future is far from certain

RESCUE

POLAR BEAR FACTS

THREATS

LOSS OF HABITAT

Climate change is the biggest threat to the polar bear. The dramatic increase in thawing of the Arctic sea ice has reduced their prey. It is predicted that the summer sea ice may disappear in the next 20 to 30 years, which will have a very bad effect on its numbers.

Polar bear fur might look white, but it actually has no colour and is transparent. It looks white because it reflects light. The large paws of a polar bear are designed to be like snowshoes. They spread out the bear's weight and stop it sinking in the snow. Its feet are also slightly webbed – like a duck's!

OIL DRILLING

Oil is already big business in the Arctic and the oil and gas industry is set to expand in the future. Polar bears can end up consuming chemicals from oil spills through grooming themselves or eating contaminated animals. Even a small amount of oil can kill a polar bear.

PREDATORS

The polar bears' only predator is man. In the past, hunting was the greatest threat to the bears but this is now restricted by the International Agreement on the Conservation of Polar Bears and their Habitat.

It's not all bad news!

The World Wildlife Fund is working to tackle climate change and stop the melting of the polar bears' sea ice habitat. They are also working to protect the Norwegian and Russian Arctic Sea from the pollution caused by shipping, fishing and oil and gas drilling.

Ben and Zoe's latest mission takes them to South Borneo. An orang-utan has set up home on a palm oil plantation and is resisting all attempts to bring him to the safety of the nearby reservation. But when they discover that illegal logging has been taking place, it becomes clear that the orang-utan isn't the only one in grave danger.

J. BURCHETT & S. VOGLER

WILD
RESCUE

SAFARI SURVIVAL

Ben and Zoe are off to the Kenyan savanna, where the population of African elephants has been fast disappearing. It seems some tourists are paying large amounts of money to hunt the creatures for 'sport', and for their latest trophy they have their sights set on a mother and baby elephant... The race is on for Ben and Zoe to track down the elephants before the hunters do.

J. BURCHETT & S. VOGLER

WILD RESCUE

OCEAN S.O.S.

Following reports that an unscrupulous marine park have dumped an unwanted young dolphin into the sea, Ben and Zoe are on their way to the Caribbean. Having been raised in captivity, the dolphin is ill-equipped for life in the open sea and soon finds itself in dangerous waters.
It's up to Ben and Zoe to guide it to safety.

If you want to find out
more about polar bears visit:

www.polarbearsinternational.org
www.wwf.org.uk